Night of the White Owls

by Anne Schraff

Perfection Learning® Corporation
Logan, Iowa 51546

Cover Design: Mark Hagenberg

Cover Image Credit: Digital Vision

For information, contact:
Perfection Learning® Corporation
1000 North Second Avenue, P.O. Box 500,
Logan, Iowa 51546-0500.
Tel: 1-800-831-4190 • Fax: 1-800-543-2745
perfectionlearning.com

Paperback ISBN 0-7891-6603-8
Reinforced Library Binding ISBN 0-7569-4708-1

1 2 3 4 5 6 PP 09 08 07 06 05

1 LILIA MARTINEZ was a 16-year-old junior at Agua Dulce High School. Her favorite subjects were English and journalism. She had written several pieces for the school literary journal, *The Sentinel.* But her most prized writing was a poem about the night white owls.

They were active tonight—the white owls—soaring through the darkness. Lilia loved to watch them from her bedroom window. They roamed over yards and under bright streetlights.

Sometimes the owls made long, quavering screeches in flight, and when Lilia heard that, she always went to the window to watch for them. But tonight something else attracted Lilia's attention. There was unusual activity at the house across the street.

Charles and Connie Spann, a couple in their forties, lived there. They had a 15-year-old daughter, Cassidy, and an 18-year-old son, Robert. Cassidy was a freshman at Agua Dulce High School, and Robert was away at college.

The Spann family had lived across the street from the Martinez family for many years. Lilia had always felt sorry for Cassidy and her brother because their parents were constantly arguing. Their noisy fights could be heard throughout the neighborhood.

Now Lilia watched as Mr. Spann lugged a very large canvas bag from the house. He half-carried, half-dragged it, until he got to the trunk of his car. Then he picked it up and shoved it into the trunk. Lilia could see the perspiration shining on his face. He was a handsome man, but bitterness had sapped his good looks. The Spanns had a terribly unhappy marriage.

A shocking, but totally ridiculous, thought came to Lilia's mind. Maybe Mr. and Mrs. Spann had had another awful fight, and Mr. Spann had killed his wife. Maybe Mrs. Spann's body was in that large bag, and Mr. Spann was carrying her away to bury her in the wilderness.

Lilia's father had often said, in jest, those two are going to kill each other one of these days if they don't stop fighting so much.

Lilia watched as Mr. Spann got into his car and drove away. Was he off to dig Mrs. Spann's grave and bury her? No, don't be silly, Lilia thought. She tried to reassure herself that the bag didn't contain a body. Perhaps Mr. Spann was cleaning out his closet and was taking some old clothes to the church. Or maybe inside the bag was a present for their son at college. Or even camping equipment. It certainly couldn't be Connie Spann.

Lilia tried to get the thought out of her mind. But as she brushed her teeth and prepared for bed, she found her thoughts continually drifting. What could be in that bag?

....

The next morning Lilia sat down for breakfast and noticed her father looking out the front window. "Connie hasn't gone to work yet," her father commented. "She's always off by the time I leave. Her car is still there. She must be sick or something."

"Oh, my," Lilia's mother replied. "I don't think I ever remember her missing work. I hope it's nothing serious."

Lilia felt strange. She remembered the night before. For a moment, Lilia wondered if what she had seen the night before had been a dream. She had been rather sleepy as she went to the window to watch the owls. But it *couldn't* have been a dream.

"Last night I saw Mr. Spann dragging a big heavy bag to his car," Lilia said. "Maybe they've gone camping." As Lilia spoke, she visualized Mr. Spann pulling the bag to his car. He almost stumbled with the weight of it.

"Oh, yeah?" her father asked. "But his car is there too. Besides, can you imagine those two roughing it in the woods?"

Lilia's mother laughed. "They both have such hot tempers. Plus, I don't think they'd handle the inconveniences too well," she said.

"I wonder why they fight so much," Lilia wondered aloud, as she spread butter on her breakfast muffin.

"Well, Charlie *is* kind of controlling,"

her mother said. "Connie told me it drives her crazy."

"I think I'll go ask Charlie if his wife is okay," Lilia's father said. He went out the front door and returned in just a few minutes.

"Connie went off to be with family for a few days," Mr. Martinez said. "Charlie didn't sound too happy about it. It seems to me they had another spat last night. He said Connie's sister picked her up."

"Strange," Lilia's mother said. "Connie is so responsible. I can't imagine her not going to work."

"Maybe Connie's family is taking her to work," Lilia's father said.

"Anyway, Charlie seemed in no mood for talking. He's never very jolly, but this morning he seemed really grumpy. So I got out of there fast. As long as Connie's all right and isn't sick or anything, whatever happened is none of our business," Lilia's father said.

Mr. Martinez glanced at his watch. "Speaking of work, I'd better get a move on. We're putting in the foundation today and I've got to make sure everything is okay."

Lilia's father had his own small construction company. Her mother taught kindergarten at the school down the street.

Lilia's mother poured herself a second cup of coffee. By now, Lilia's twin sisters, ten-year old Dina and Elvira, were having breakfast too. The twins always got a ride to school from their mother, but Lilia caught the bus to Agua Dulce.

"You know what, Mom?" Lilia said nervously. "I told you guys I saw Mr. Spann carrying a heavy bag to his car last night. I wonder what that was?"

"Well, they get rid of clothes as soon as they go out of style! Almost-new things are off to the thrift store. Even Cassidy's things," her mother said.

Cassidy! Lilia had almost forgotten about her. Lilia resolved to talk to her at school to make sure everything was okay.

"Yeah, clothes were probably in that bag, Mom," Lilia said.

As Lilia waited for the school bus, she thought about the Spanns. They had lived across the street for many years. In the beginning they had come to the neighborhood barbecues. Then they stopped coming. Once, a long time ago, Cassidy had come to Lilia's birthday party. But it seemed as time went by, the Spann family grew more reclusive. They were still ordinary people, though, Lilia thought to herself. And ordinary people don't commit murder and put bodies in canvas bags. Or do they?

When Lilia got on the bus she noticed her friend Holly Suarez. Lilia sat down next to her.

"Hi, Holly!" Lilia said.

"What's new?" Holly asked.

"Oh, nothing," Lilia replied, then she hesitated. "Cassidy's mom, you know, across the street . . . she didn't go to work today. I guess the Spann family had another fight last night."

Holly gave Lilia a funny look as if to say, "Who cares?" It wasn't exactly earthshaking news that Connie Spann skipped work. So Lilia added, "Mr. Spann was acting kind of weird last night, dragging junk to the car and stuff . . . "

"Poor Cassidy. She seems like such a loner," Holly said. "I've seen her dad yelling at her when he drops her off at school."

"Holly, you know those owls I told you about that live on my street?" Lilia asked.

"Uh huh," Holly said disinterestedly. She was watching a guy on a motorcycle. He was new at school. His name was Joel Zapata, and Holly thought he was cute.

"Well," Lilia continued, "last night I was watching the owls, and then I noticed Mr. Spann pulling this really heavy canvas bag to his car. And he put it in the trunk. Well, don't laugh at me or anything, but I thought maybe . . . well, the way those people fight and stuff . . . I mean, I know it's totally crazy, but you know what I thought?" Lilia laughed nervously. "I thought maybe Mrs. Spann was in that bag. Isn't that the craziest thing you've ever heard?"

Holly stared at Lilia. "That *is* off the wall," she said.

Lilia was embarrassed that she had even mentioned it. "I guess I have a weird imagination. But he was struggling so hard with that bag, and this morning his wife didn't go to work. And that family does have a history of arguing," she said.

"The bag was probably full of stuff he was taking to the cleaners," Holly said.

"Maybe," Lilia said, "but the way Mr. Spann was dragging it made it seem like the bag was heavy."

"Connie Spann drives that cool car, doesn't she?" Holly asked, quickly changing the subject. "I wonder what a car like that would cost. I'd sure like to have one."

"Costs a ton of money," Lilia said.

"When we start to drive, maybe we could go buy one together. A used one," Holly said.

As the school bus neared Agua Dulce, Lilia turned to Holly. "I'm going to talk to Cassidy today and make sure everything is cool."

"Come on, Lilia, you're getting carried away with your imagination," Holly said.

"I know. But all the time I was watching last night, I was thinking wouldn't it be awful if his wife was in that bag? I couldn't stop thinking about it," Lilia said.

A look of horror touched Holly's face.

"You're serious about this, aren't you? I mean, you're really serious!" she said.

2 AFTER THE BUS DROPPED the girls off, Lilia looked around for Cassidy Spann. She was usually with other freshmen outside the algebra classroom at this hour. Lilia was eager to see Cassidy to put her own mind at ease. If Cassidy was all right, then nothing horrible could have happened in her house the night before.

Or was it possible that Cassidy had slept through the terrible fight? She had told Lilia once she went to sleep with headphones on, listening to music. So, if her father had hurt her mother and carried her away, Cassidy might not have even known.

Lilia searched and searched, but couldn't find Cassidy among the other freshmen. "See, Holly?" Lilia said, "Cassidy isn't here. That looks suspicious . . ."

"Maybe she went with her mother somewhere. Or maybe she's just late," Holly said. "Oh, look! There's Joel Zapata. Isn't he cute?"

Lilia turned around. Joel was tall with black curly hair and beautiful blue eyes. He was a junior, but he was 17. He was a transfer student who had been at Agua Dulce High School for just a month. His family had moved from northern to southern California. Everybody—especially the girls—noticed him immediately. Not only was he handsome, but he had a cool polish about him.

Lilia thought she would pass out if he showed an interest in her. She didn't expect it would happen. A guy who looked like that had too many opportunities!

But then, to Lilia's shock, Joel came walking over. "Lilia, I saw your poem in *The Sentinel*. It was good. Usually I hate those poems because they're sappy, but yours was funny and sharp."

"Uh, thanks," Lilia said, beaming inside.

Writing for the school journal was one of Lilia's favorite things to do. She was thrilled that somebody had taken notice. But at the same time, she was surprised it was Joel! They had never really spoken before. Lilia hadn't even thought, until now, that he knew who she was.

Lilia turned and walked away, and Holly grabbed her arm. "You lucky thing, Lilia. Did you see how he smiled at you?"

"Oh, it's not me he likes. It's the poem," Lilia said.

When they were in Mr. Villalobos's English class, Holly kept nudging Lilia and informing her that Joel was glancing at her frequently.

"Girls," Mr. Villalobos finally said, "once you're caught up on your social chatter, maybe you could turn your attention to *The Great Gatsby*. This novel will be featured prominently on our next exam."

The bell rang, and Lilia rushed to the cafeteria for lunch. She wanted to sit at her favorite table with Holly and their friend Meghan. Lilia had temporarily forgotten about the Spann family and was thinking about Joel Zapata instead. Although Lilia knew she was sort of pretty, she didn't think she was nearly attractive enough to get the serious attention of a boy like Joel.

Suddenly Joel was at Lilia's table. "This

place taken?" he asked, standing behind an empty chair at the table.

"No," Lilia said.

"Good," Joel said, sitting down with his tray. "So, you guys, are the tamales good today? I took a burrito. Usually they're better. Not good, but better."

"The tamales are okay," Lilia said.

Joel smiled. His eyes glowed. "When I read your poem in *The Sentinel* and I found out you were in my class, I thought, I've got to meet this girl," Joel said. "I write too. I write comedy skits. I perform sometimes in little clubs."

"Oh, that's great," Lilia said. "So how do you like Agua Dulce High School?"

"Good. Pretty good. It's much smaller than my old school. I'm not saying my old school was jam-packed. But let's put it this way—my shoulders used to be 20 inches across, but now they're 16 inches. That's from fighting my way to the lockers," Joel said.

The three girls laughed. Lilia felt herself getting a little more comfortable with Joel.

"Hey, this is one dry burrito," Joel said, adding salsa.

"Not like our moms make, huh?" Holly said.

"Actually, my father makes better burritos and tamales than my mom does," Joel said. "I'm not saying Mom's a bad cook or anything, but when I have friends over, they brown-bag it."

Lilia giggled.

"You get the cutest dimple in your face when you laugh, Lilia. Did anybody ever tell you that?" Joel asked.

Lilia felt her face turning warm. "No," she said.

"Your eyes sparkle too," Joel said. "When you laugh your whole face laughs."

Lilia's face got warmer. She struggled for something to say. "I don't think I've ever met anybody who's a comedian before. That must be so fun," she finally said.

"Yeah, well, you know what they say— laugh and the world laughs with you, cry and you cry alone," Joel said. "This Friday night I'm trying out a new monologue at Club Jupiter. Maybe you guys would like to come and watch me make a fool of myself."

Club Jupiter was a place where teens

could dance and enjoy snacks and sodas. Usually a DJ provided the entertainment, but sometimes the club hosted young performers. Lilia had been there a couple of times, and she had always had fun.

"I'd love to go," Lilia said.

"Me too," Holly said. "I like to laugh."

"Count me in," Meghan said. "My brother can drive us."

"Great," Joel said. "At least there'll be a few people not throwing tomatoes at me when I lay an egg."

When the lunch period ended, Lilia wondered if Joel had been putting on an act just so he could have some fans at Club Jupiter for Friday. He had probably noticed that Lilia had a lot of friends and thought if he threw her a couple of compliments, she would bring a rooting section for him on Friday. Maybe that was the only reason he was acting nice and friendly. But Lilia did not really mind. It was exciting to be friends with Joel Zapata for any reason.

"We'll laugh our heads off at Club Jupiter and make Joel look good, huh, Holly? Even though the guy was ignoring us completely and drooling over Lilia here," Meghan said.

"Yeah," Holly said. "Even if Joel's act is terrible, we will still laugh. But only because we're friends with you, Lilia."

"You guys," Lilia said, "he doesn't like me any better than he likes anybody else."

"Oh yeah, right," Meghan said, "and lemons aren't really sour either."

That afternoon, Lilia rode the bus home without Meghan or Holly because both girls were staying after school for swim team tryouts. As Lilia neared her neighborhood, she thought about the Spann family again. She hoped Mrs. Spann would be home, and everything would be normal again.

When Lilia got off the bus, she saw Mrs. Spann's car parked just as it had been that morning. Lilia also noticed Mr. Spann standing in his front yard staring into space. Usually he was not home from work at this time. He put in a lot of overtime hours at his job.

"Hi, Mr. Spann," Lilia called out as she passed his house before she started across the street. Mr. Spann was never very friendly. Usually he greeted the neighbors in a very brief way.

"Hello," he said, frowning.

"Cassidy wasn't in school today," Lilia said. "Is she okay?"

"Yes," he said, turning and going back inside his house. He closed the door with a slam.

Elvira came out as Lilia walked toward the house. "That guy gives me the creeps, sis," Elvira said. "Ever since we got home from school, he's just been standing there in his yard. Like he's looking for something."

"That's weird," Lilia said. "He hardly ever comes out in the yard. They've got the gardener to keep the yard in good shape. I never see anybody from that family looking at their own flowers."

Lilia had no intention of sharing with her little sister what she had seen the night before. So she motioned for Elvira to follow her into the house. The girls enjoyed an after-school snack, then Lilia sat down to do her homework.

When Lilia's father came home around 7:00, Lilia joined him in the yard before he went inside for dinner.

"Dad, I need to tell you something," Lilia said.

"Okay, shoot," her father said in a lighthearted way.

"Dad, I'm probably just being stupid. But last night when I was watching the white owls flying from the palm trees, I saw Mr. Spann dragging a bag to his car. It looked like it was heavy. He put it in the trunk, and then he drove away," Lilia said.

"So?" her father asked. "I load up my car all the time and take stuff to the rummage sale at church. What are you getting at, Lilia?"

"Well, Mrs. Spann didn't go to work today . . . and . . . Cassidy wasn't in school. I mean they're fighting so bitterly all the time. You've even said they're going to kill each other one of these days . . ." Lilia's voice trailed.

Her father started to laugh. "Oh Lilia! I'm joking when I talk like that. Surely you don't take me seriously! You know, the Spanns are not like us, but they're still nice, decent people. You think Charlie was carrying Connie's body in that bag? Is that what you're saying? Lilia! Shame on you for even thinking such a thing. I think you've been watching too many mystery movies on television!"

It annoyed Lilia that her father was laughing at her. Even if the Spann family seemed normal, they could still do bad things.

"Dad, regular people who seem nice are doing awful things all the time. Do you think people look different if they're evil? Besides, where *is* Mrs. Spann?"

"Honey, Charlie told me she was staying with family. He said everything was all right. The Spanns are very private people. They don't share their lives with neighbors, and that's all right. They have a right to their privacy." Lilia's father started to chuckle again. "Oh, my, did you really think Connie was in that bag Mr. Spann was carrying last night? Lilia, you should write mystery stories like that English lady of long ago—that Agatha Christie."

"Well," Lilia sniffed. "I'm not so sure there isn't something wrong over there!"

Lilia's father threw his arm around her shoulder as they walked toward the house. "Don't worry, there is no murderer living across the street from us. Just the battling Spanns. They are noisy sometimes, but harmless."

That night, Lilia stood at her bedroom window watching the owls again. They were swimming in the darkness, then diving when they spotted a rodent. From time to time Lilia glanced at the Spann house. It was usually lit up at this time of night, but tonight, the bedrooms were dark.

Suddenly, a tow truck pulled up to the house. Two men got out and talked to Mr. Spann for a few minutes. Then they started loading Mrs. Spann's car onto the bed of the truck, securing it in place.

Lilia ran from her bedroom to her parents' room. "Mom! Dad!" she cried. "They're towing Mrs. Spann's car away. That means she won't need it anymore! Don't you understand?"

Lilia's father looked startled. "Are you sure they're towing it away for good?"

"Dad, just look out the window! Mr. Spann is getting rid of that car his wife loved so much!" Lilia said. "He knows she won't need it anymore!"

3   "WELL, I'LL BE DARNED," Lilia's
    father said when he got to the
    window.

"We need to do something," Lilia
pleaded. "Maybe we should call the police."

"Hold on," her father said. "There might
be a perfectly good explanation. Wouldn't
we feel foolish if there was mechanical
trouble with the car? Perhaps they're just
towing it to a garage to be serviced."

Lilia's father was still dressed, so he
and Lilia went downstairs. They crossed
the street as the tow-truck men were
winding up the job of securing the car.

"Problems with the car, Mr. Spann?"
Lilia's father asked in an amiable,
nonthreatening voice. Mr. Spann turned
toward them, a hostile look on his face.
He clearly resented the intrusion into his
business.

"My wife doesn't want the car anymore.
I'm selling it," he said.

"But Mrs. Spann loves that car," Lilia

cried. "She was so proud of it. She took me for a ride in it once."

Mr. Spann looked even more annoyed. "She changed her mind. She has changed her mind about a lot of things. I'm sorry to say that we're separated. We're getting a divorce. That's what she told me anyway. She and our daughter have gone off. You must excuse me now. I have papers to fill out," he said.

"Yes, of course," Lilia's father said. "I'm real sorry, Charlie. I hope things turn around for you."

Lilia and her father turned and walked back to their house. "Dad, do you believe him?"

"Of course I believe him. People are getting divorced all the time. There's nothing unusual about that. In fact, given the fighting in that house, I'm surprised it took so long for that to happen. The one I feel sorry for is Cassidy. It's going to be rough on her," Lilia's father replied.

....

On Friday night, Lilia and her friends went to Club Jupiter to watch Joel. He came out on stage wearing dark jeans and a T-shirt with the name of a band on it. Lilia, Holly, and Meghan had good seats up front. When the spotlight hit Joel, they looked at one another and grinned.

"Whoa, he's cute," Holly sighed.

"Yeah," Meghan said with mock bitterness. "Let's take Lilia out in a boat and drown her. Then maybe Joel will forget about her."

"Shhh. He's about to start," Lilia said.

The girls cheered loudly as Joel was introduced. As he began his comedy routine, the girls could not help but laugh. He really was quite good, and Lilia could tell the audience agreed by their laughter.

"Wow," said Holly midway through the act. "He's pretty funny! I'm glad we came!"

After the show, Lilia went backstage to tell Joel how funny he was.

"Thanks," Joel said. "I guess the boss here agrees with you. He asked me to come back next Friday. He said it's unusual to have an act back two weeks in a row, so I guess that means I didn't do too bad. Hey, you'll be here next Friday won't you, Lilia?"

"I'm not sure. My grandmother is having a birthday party. The big 60. It's kind of special. Everybody is coming. So I might not be able to get away Friday night," Lilia said.

"Aww, you wouldn't miss my show for a grandmother's birthday party, would you?" Joel asked. "Go early, hang the gift on her walker, and then split, okay?"

"Joel, my grandmother is only 60. She doesn't need a walker! Her mother is 82, and she doesn't need a walker either," Lilia said in an annoyed voice.

"Okay, but you've got to come on Friday. You've just got to. You're my good-luck charm," Joel said.

"I'll sure try," Lilia promised.

Lilia motioned for her friends to join her, and the three girls left the club.

"Joel really likes you, Lilia. I caught him lots of times during his act looking right at you and smiling," Holly said.

Lilia smiled. She felt a strong chemistry between herself and Joel. At 16½, Lilia had had some boys who were friends, but she had never had a serious boyfriend. Maybe this was it. Maybe this incredibly handsome boy was going to be her first real boyfriend.

"So what's happening with your weird neighbor?" Holly asked, as the girls piled into the car. "Any sign of the missing wife and daughter yet?"

"Mr. Spann told my dad that he and his wife are getting a divorce. He also said that Cassidy is with her mom," Lilia said.

"That's sad," said Holly. "Cassidy must be having a hard time."

"Yeah, probably," said Lilia.

Meghan's brother dropped Lilia off at her house, and she stood for a moment waving to her friends. It was only 9:30.

Lilia glanced over at the Spann house, and it made her sad. Poor Cassidy. It had to be so hard on her. Lilia couldn't imagine how she would feel if something like that were happening in her family.

Mr. Spann came out of his house then, and Lilia ducked behind the shrubbery in her yard. He was carrying a box that he emptied into the trash container at the curb. Whatever he was throwing into the container made a lot of noise. Lilia heard crashing and crunching sounds like pottery or china was breaking.

When Mr. Spann went back inside the

house, Lilia went over to see what was in the trash container. She knew she shouldn't be sifting through the neighbor's trash, but she was curious about what he was throwing away.

"Ohhhh," Lilia gasped. She stared at the crushed fragments of Mrs. Spann's beloved Christmas elf collection from Bavaria. Lilia knew how much Connie Spann treasured the collection. There must have been at least 50 of the 2½-inch-tall ceramic elves. Each Christmas Mrs. Spann displayed them around the house. There had been a few times when Cassidy had taken Lilia into the house when her parents weren't home to show her the elves. Lilia remembered Cassidy sharing how much her mother loved those Christmas decorations.

What on earth was Mr. Spann thinking of to savagely hurl the precious elves into the trash, making sure to break them into as many pieces as possible?

Suddenly he was there, glaring at Lilia in the darkness. "You!" he hissed. "How dare you come snooping in my trash? I am appalled!"

"I—I'm sorry," Lilia gasped, too shocked by the malicious destruction of the elves to be afraid, "but why did you do this? Your wife loved those! Why would you smash them like that?"

"It's none of your business! How dare you intrude on my privacy like this?" Mr. Spann snarled.

"But . . . it's just so awful," Lilia stammered.

"Do you think I owe you an explanation? Are they yours? I can do what I wish with anything in my house. My wife has lost interest in the stupid elves, as she has lost interest in the marriage. They are merely dust catchers now, and I have no use for them. Who would want them? Ugly, twisted little wretches. Only a fool like Connie would have spent good money on such nonsense. Are you satisfied now, Lilia? Have I given you enough of an explanation for you to go home where you belong?" Mr. Spann's voice dripped with sarcasm.

Lilia hurried across the street to her own house. When she walked into the

living room, her parents were watching
television.

"Do you know what he did?" Lilia cried.
"Mr. Spann smashed all his wife's cute
little Bavarian Christmas elves and put
them in the trash."

Lilia's mother looked up, shocked. She
collected cute little ceramics too, usually
kittens doing playful things. Once in a
while, she and Connie would shop
together for their collections. "Lilia! I can't
believe that. Are you sure?" her mother
asked.

"I saw them all broken and crushed in
his trash," Lilia said. "He caught me, and
he was really nasty."

"Honey," her father scolded, "it's rude
to look at other people's trash."

"I know," Lilia said. "But there he was
hurling the stuff into the container, and I
heard these smashing sounds. He
violently threw them in, one by one, to
make sure they were all destroyed. His
eyes were brimming with hatred. I have
never seen a man look so awful in my life,
like he was capable of anything!"

"Poor Connie," Lilia's mother groaned,

"she is going to be so devastated when she finds out what he did. What a cruel, vindictive thing. He had no right to destroy her stuff.

"You know, Luis, I always hated the controlling way he treated her. But this takes the cake—smashing those little elves that were so dear to her. Connie is going to be furious, and I don't blame her."

Maybe not, Lilia thought grimly. Maybe Connie Spann will never know that her elves were destroyed. Maybe before Mr. Spann crushed the elves he crushed her . . . and carried her off in that large bag to lie in a shallow grave.

4 "YOU GUYS," LILIA SAID, "would Mr. Spann have had the nerve to be smashing all those elves if he knew his wife was going to find out?"

Lilia's father glanced at her mother. Lilia had already told her father that she suspected Mr. Spann had murdered his wife. But neither Lilia nor her father had shared this suspicion with Lilia's mother.

"Lilia has these suspicions that maybe Connie Spann is dead, Carla," Lilia's father began.

"Dead? Why would she be dead? The last time I saw her she was fine!" Lilia's mother said.

"Mom," Lilia said, "remember the other morning when we saw her car in the driveway when she should have been at work?"

"Yes," her mother said, looking bewildered.

"And, remember when I told you I saw Mr. Spann dragging a heavy bag out to his car? Which happened to be the night before we discovered Mrs. Spann's car still in the driveway?" Lilia asked.

Her mother's eyes widened, and she looked a little pale. "You're not saying you think Mrs. Spann was . . . in that bag, are you?" she asked in a trembling voice.

"Kind of," Lilia admitted.

"Oh, Lilia," her mother said, "That is so horrible. I won't believe that for a minute!"

"But he's gotten rid of her car. She loved that car. And now he smashed her elf collection. I mean, he claims they're separated and they're getting divorced. But if that's true, why would he dare get rid of all her stuff?" Lilia asked.

Her mother clasped her hands to her cheeks. "Oh, my goodness. Wouldn't it be terrible if something like that did happen? If they were fighting and he hit her or something and she died . . . and he took her off to bury her . . . " she said.

"Shouldn't we be doing something?" Lilia demanded. "I mean, do we just sit here and keep quiet?"

"When I spoke with Mr. Spann the other

night, he claimed his wife and daughter were staying with family. I don't know any of Mrs. Spann's family or I'd call them," Lilia's father said. "And, come to think of it, I don't think I've seen other family members over there . . ."

"We've got to call the police!" Lilia cried.

"I don't feel right intruding on their business," her father began. "It just doesn't seem right to call the police."

"I know," Lilia said. "Cassidy has a good friend at school—Ashley. If Cassidy is okay she would have called Ashley. I'll ask Ashley at school on Monday if she's heard anything. If not, then surely something is wrong. Then we will call the police so they can search for evidence before Mr. Spann has gotten rid of everything."

When Lilia got to school on Monday, she looked for Ashley. Lilia wasn't best friends with Cassidy or Ashley, but she saw them every day and always said hi. Lilia had noticed that Ashley and Cassidy were inseparable. They did everything together. Lilia never saw one without the other. Lilia felt like kicking herself for not contacting Ashley before now.

"Hey, Ashley," Lilia called when she saw the girl.

"Hi," Ashley said. She was a lot like Cassidy, quiet and a little sad looking most of the time.

"Ashley, I live across the street from Cassidy, and I haven't seen her or her mom for several days. My family is getting worried. Has Cassidy called you?" Lilia asked.

"Her parents are getting divorced," Ashley said in a forlorn voice. "Cass's parents are splitting. She called me last Tuesday night and told me. Cass said it was war all the time but now it's over. She said she had never heard them fight as bad as they did last Tuesday. She said her mom was leaving her dad. Cass was crying real hard. Anyway, she said she'd get in touch with me, but she hasn't . . . "

"Mr. Spann said his wife and Cassidy are staying with family," Lilia said. "Do you know where their family lives?"

Ashley shook her head. "Cass never

talked much about relatives. She and I are really close, but Cass's father is strange. He never let anybody come over and visit. Kids could never go there. And he didn't want Cassidy talking about family stuff. One time he found out that Cass had told me about a fight her parents had, and he grounded Cass for a month," she said.

Lilia did not want to say any more. If she even hinted what she feared, it would be all over Agua Dulce in an hour. She didn't want to start a horrible rumor. Everybody would be saying that Cassidy and her mother had been murdered by Mr. Spann. And maybe that was totally wrong. So all Lilia said was, "If you hear from Cassidy, let me know, Ashley."

"I will. I'm worried too. I don't know why she hasn't called me. We're like sisters. I hope she's okay," Ashley said.

"Yeah," Lilia agreed.

"You know, Cassidy's father made a to-do list for her every day. She had to do stuff, and then at night, he'd check the things off the list. He used to give her demerits when she didn't do something. One time she was supposed to do the ironing and she didn't. He made her scrub the kitchen floor with a toothbrush. It was late, like 11:00 at night, and he made her do that. He did stuff like that to his wife too. He was like a commanding officer, and he treated his family like the soldiers. He even inspected Cassidy every morning to make sure she was dressed the way he liked. I think Cassidy's father is really weird," Ashley said.

When Lilia got home from school, she told her parents what Ashley had said. "I think we need to call the police," Lilia said. "I think something awful has happened over there."

Lilia's father took a deep breath. "Well, first I'm going to talk to Charlie Spann, man to man. I'm going to lay it on the line about our concerns. Maybe he'll give me the phone number of where Connie and Cassidy are staying. Then we can call over there and put our minds at ease. If he acts suspicious and refuses to play ball, then we'll call the police," Lilia's dad said.

Lilia's father walked across the street alone and rang the Spann doorbell. Lilia watched from the open front window as

Mr. Spann opened the door. He did not invite Lilia's father into the house, so the entire conversation floated across the street where Lilia and her mother could hear most of it.

"Charlie," Lilia's father said, "I know you're a very private man, and we don't want to intrude on you, but we're very worried about Connie."

"I told you she left me," Mr. Spann snapped.

"Yes, you did, but then we see her car being towed away and my daughter said Connie's ceramic elf collection was smashed and thrown in the trash. It just sounds ominous. To add to the mystery, Cassidy has dropped out of school. It's like something dire happened to the two of them," Lilia's father continued.

"She left me," Mr. Spann said. "And she took our daughter."

"Charlie, you said she went to stay with family. If you would just give me the phone number, then I could talk to Connie and make sure everything is all right. Then I swear my family won't bother you again. We just want to make sure that your wife and Cassidy are okay," Lilia's father said.

"This is an outrage," Mr. Spann said hotly. "You have no right to come over here and question me as if I were a criminal. Who do you think you are, Martinez?"

"Charlie, calm down. If you'd just give me the phone number . . ." Lilia's father said.

"I don't have it," Mr. Spann snapped. "I have never had anything to do with Connie's family. They're a bed of vipers. They've hated me from the beginning. They have wanted to break up this marriage from day one."

"Look, Charlie, we're afraid that Connie and your daughter have been harmed. We haven't seen them for days. And you're disposing of all your wife's possessions as if you're sure she won't ever come back for them. We can't just stand by and ignore it. If you can't put me in touch with your wife and daughter, then we'll have no choice but to call the police," Lilia's father said in a calm but stern voice.

A stream of angry curses flew from

Charlie Spann's lips. He wheeled around and rushed back inside the house, slamming the door behind him.

By this time, Dina and Elvira knew what was going on too. When their father came home, Elvira demanded, "Did Mr. Spann hurt his wife?"

"We don't know," Lilia's mother replied.

"I saw him hit her once," Dina said, almost shamefacedly, as if to have witnessed such a thing was wrong and only to be spoken of in whispers. "She was taking shopping bags from the car, and he came out and he didn't like that she'd bought so much. He hit her in the face . . ."

Lilia's father looked like he was carrying the weight of the world on his shoulders as he moved toward the telephone. "I think we have to call the police," he said. "It would be wrong if we didn't. Everything might be okay, but if it isn't, we'd never forgive ourselves. The police will find Connie if she's okay, and if not . . . well, they'll start searching for her . . ."

Lilia watched her father dial the police.

He hated so much to do this. He fiercely respected the privacy of other people. He was torn between strong emotions. He was making serious trouble for a neighbor who perhaps had enough trouble without this. Maybe Mr. Spann had been abandoned by his family and he was distraught. Or maybe Lilia's father was exposing a murder while there was still evidence to collect.

Lilia walked to her father's side as he dialed, leaning against him and hugging him. "We have to, Daddy," she whispered, to give him courage.

After explaining the situation to the police, Lilia's father got off the phone. "The police said they would look into the matter," he said sadly.

THE NEXT EVENING as Lilia's family ate dinner, they turned on the TV to watch the local evening news.

"Sssh," Lilia's father ordered. "I think something is going to be on about the Spann family."

The news reporter began. "Connie Spann and her daughter, Cassidy, 15, have been reported missing by the husband and father of the pair, Charles Spann. According to Mr. Spann, the two vanished after a family argument. Mrs. Spann, a legal secretary and homemaker, left the family home around 10:00 last Tuesday, but she did not take her automobile. Mr. Spann believes his wife and daughter were picked up by a relative. Police are asking anyone with information about the whereabouts of Connie or her daughter, Cassidy, to call local law enforcement."

"Well," Lilia's father said, "looks like the police have gotten involved. And apparently Charlie has convinced the police he doesn't know where his wife and daughter are. It's being treated as a missing persons case."

"If Mrs. Spann and Cassidy really are missing, then why didn't Mr. Spann report them missing right away?" Lilia asked. "Why did he wait until we called the police?"

Lilia's mother shook her head. "Let's not rush to judgment, Lilia. They had a fight and Connie took off with Cassidy. Maybe Charlie thought they'd hide out for a few days and then surface. But it's been a week now," her mom said.

"If we hadn't called the police, he never would have said anything," Lilia said. "I don't believe they're missing at all. I think he knows where they are!"

....

In school the next day, Joel Zapata joined Lilia as she was eating lunch. Holly and Meghan were practicing with the glee club, so they couldn't make it.

"Well, at least the three musketeers split up long enough to let me sneak in," Joel said.

"When we all eat lunch, just join us," Lilia said. "You don't have to be shy about it."

"One thing I never am is shy," Joel said. "But it's nicer when it's just the two of us. They're okay, your friends, but I like you alone."

Lilia felt a little uncomfortable. Joel was coming on a bit too strong.

"You really intrigue me," Joel said.

Lilia laughed nervously. "There's nothing about me that's intriguing. I'm pretty ordinary. I'm just a 16-year-old . . . "

Joel cut into her words before she could finish. "Don't sell yourself short. You're pretty and interesting. I've gone to several high schools and I've never met a girl as special as you. The first time I saw you, I knew I had to get to know you better."

Lilia was even more uncomfortable now. She was flattered by his attention, but it made her uneasy that he seemed to like her so much, so quickly. "Well, I think you're pretty special too, Joel, but . . ." she said.

"You're coming to my gig on Friday, right?" Joel asked. "I'm counting on it."

"I think so. My grandmother will understand that I have to leave early," Lilia said.

"Yeah, tell your granny that you're a big girl now, and you have to do your own thing," Joel said.

"Joel, you don't understand how it is with our family. I wouldn't hurt her feelings for the world. Family is very big with me," Lilia said.

Joel smiled thinly and finished his macaroni and string beans.

When Lilia got together with Holly and Meghan after school, she said, "Joel ate lunch with me today. He said I was intriguing, but that's so stupid. He's such a handsome guy. I bet all kinds of girls are falling over him. Why is he interested in me?"

"Because you're pretty," Holly said. "I'd give anything to have those big green eyes, that cute little oval face, and above all, that size 6 figure!"

Meghan was tall and willowy and always wished she could be a bit shorter. "Yeah, I'd just like to be five foot four!" she said ruefully.

"You guys, stop it! I'm no prettier than either one of you or any of the girls at Agua Dulce. I just don't get it. I like Joel, but he gives me the creeps when he comes on like that. I mean, he's only a year older than me, but he acts so mature," Lilia said.

"Oh, stop complaining," Holly laughed. "He's such a hunk you ought to be on your knees in thanksgiving!"

"I'm not complaining," Lilia said, "but it's just strange . . . "

"Speaking of strange," Meghan said, "I saw your missing neighbors on TV last night. I guess Cass and her mom just ran away from home. Maybe they're hiding out now because they're scared of Mr. Spann."

"Maybe," Lilia said. She had heard of women who had gone to battered women's shelters and hidden their whereabouts from abusive husbands. But surely if that had happened in this case, the authorities would have found out. The police would have checked the shelters before they put out the missing persons alert.

....

Lilia went to her grandmother's party after school on Friday. The church hall was crowded with cousins and aunts and uncles. Two people played guitars while others sang and danced. It was a big occasion because Lilia's grandma was turning 60. The milestones that occurred every decade were celebrated by the Martinez family with even more fanfare than regular birthday parties.

Lilia got so absorbed in the party, talking to her cousins, that she lost track of time. When she glanced at her watch she realized it was 7:00. Joel was scheduled to perform at Club Jupiter at 7:30. Lilia kissed her grandmother good-bye and gave her a gift. Then Lilia asked her cousin to drive her to the night club.

"You really know a guy who's performing there?" Manuel, Lilia's cousin, asked as they drove. "That's pretty cool."

"Yeah, I go to school with him. Joel Zapata. He's a comedian," Lilia said.

"Great. I love to laugh," Manuel said.

Lilia and Manuel couldn't get very good

seats because they were late. They were pretty far back from the stage. When Joel came out and stepped into the spotlight, he seemed to be looking around for somebody. Lilia tried to make eye contact with him and smile, but she wasn't sure if he saw her.

The audience roared loudly at Joel's jokes, which were mostly put-downs of girls and women. Lilia wished he'd aim some of his comedy barbs at guys too, but Manuel and most of the other guys in the club were doubled over laughing. Because Joel was so handsome, the girls forgave him for his abrasive monologue, and some of them were laughing too.

"He's good," Manuel said after Joel left the stage. "He looks a little bit like that guy who used to be on TV—the one who had the big sitcom. Just think, if he gets a sitcom one day, you can say that you know him!"

The show ended, but there was too much of a crowd to get to see Joel, so Lilia decided to wait until Monday to see him and tell him how funny he was.

....

On Saturday mid-morning, several police cars pulled up to the Spann house. The police entered the house. Two hours later, the police emerged carrying boxes. Each box was placed in a squad car. During the entire ordeal, Mr. Spann paced outside on his front lawn. He seemed furious.

Cold chills ran up Lilia's spine as she watched the police bustling around. "I think they suspect that he killed her," she finally said to her parents. "Why would they be over there searching if they didn't suspect something?"

"That doesn't mean he did it though. Yeah, they're suspicious, but the search might clear him," Lilia's dad said.

Eventually the police left. Mr. Spann stood outside his house. Lilia's mother peered out the front window nervously. "Look at him! Look at that angry man over there glaring in our direction! I bet he blames us for everything. Oh, Luis, I feel so frightened. If he did harm his wife and daughter then . . . he's a murderer. And he lives right across the street from us! Why don't the police take him away?" she asked.

"The police might not have enough evidence," Lilia's father said. "He might be innocent, you know."

"He had a week and a half to get rid of the evidence," Lilia said. "A whole week and a half to destroy proof of what he did!"

6 MONDAY, JUST AFTER Lilia arrived at school, Joel walked over. It was obvious he had been waiting for her. "Hi, Joel," Lilia said. "You were really good on Friday. I wanted to tell you in person, but there was such a big crowd waiting to see you."

Joel didn't smile. He looked almost angry. "I was really disappointed when I came out and you weren't there," he said.

"I *was* there with my cousin. We saw the whole show. We were sort of in the back though. I guess the word got around how funny you are, so more people came this time. It was harder to get a good seat," Lilia said.

"I just don't understand why you didn't get there earlier," Joel said. "You knew how important it was to me."

Lilia was getting annoyed at his attitude. "Joel, I told you I had to go to my grandmother's birthday party. That was important too. I did the best I could," she said.

"Okay," Joel said, finally easing up. "See you at lunch, huh?"

"Sure," Lilia said. She was sorry Joel was upset that she got to Club Jupiter late, but she couldn't understand why he was making such a big deal of it. He's weird, she thought. He's talented and handsome, but there's something strange about him.

The lunch hour soon arrived, and Lilia raced to the cafeteria. She sat down at her usual table and looked for Holly and Meghan. They were nowhere to be found. But Joel was there on time, walking over with his tray and sitting opposite Lilia.

"Spaghetti and meatballs today, eh?" he asked, seeming to have gotten over his temper tantrum. "I can't see how they could miss with spaghetti and meatballs!"

"Not enough meatballs," Lilia said, grinning.

"Oh, right," Joel said, "I should have known. They skimped on the meatballs. So, Lilia, you really thought I was funny on Friday?"

Lilia wanted to be honest, but the truth was that Joel's monologue on Friday night was mean and sarcastic. It was much different than the first time she had seen him perform. But to spare Joel's feelings, Lilia simply said, "I thought it was great! You were really good."

"Yeah?" Joel said. "You really liked it, huh?"

"Yes. Everybody around me was laughing too," Lilia said.

She decided to change the subject. "Something weird is happening in our neighborhood. The lady across the street and her daughter have vanished. Maybe you saw something about it on TV. The daughter goes to high school here."

"I think I did see something on TV about missing people," Joel said, taking a long drink of his soda. "Hey, Lilia, would you like to go to the movies with me on Friday? There's a great old Woody Allen film showing—a classic from ages ago. It's really funny. I get a lot of my ideas from movies like that."

"I don't know, Joel. I'll let you know if I'm free," Lilia said. She was a little put off that Joel appeared disinterested in the missing woman and her daughter. It seemed like he was self-centered.

"I'd love for you to come, Lilia," Joel pressed. "Try to make it."

As Lilia walked to her English class, she noticed Holly and Meghan walking ahead of her. "Hey, you guys," Lilia called out. "Where were you at lunch?"

The two girls looked at each other, then Meghan said, "Lilia, what kind of a question is that? Joel told us you guys wanted to be alone for lunch. That you had stuff to talk about."

"What?" Lilia gasped. "I don't know what you're talking about. I was looking for you guys at lunch!"

The girls looked at each other again. Then Holly spoke up. "Lilia, Joel came up to us right before lunch. He said that Meghan and I should skip out on lunch today because you two needed to talk. He said it was private."

"I can't believe he did that!" Lilia fumed. "Do you guys really think I'd ask you not to eat lunch with me?"

"Well," Meghan said, "he is a hunk."

"Yeah," Holly agreed, "and it wouldn't be the first time a girl forgot her girlfriends when a boy came into the picture."

"Well, that's not me," Lilia snapped. "It really bothers me that he would do something like that."

Later, when Lilia saw Joel walking to his motorcycle after school, she caught up to him. "Joel, why did you tell Holly and Meghan not to come eat lunch with us?" she asked.

"I wanted you all to myself. If that's a crime, shoot me!" He grinned as he spoke.

"Joel, I kind of resent you doing that. They're *my* friends. I mean, I've known those girls all my life. I would never want to hurt their feelings like that," Lilia said.

"Hey, it's not a big deal, is it?" Joel asked.

"Yes, it is a big deal. I'm an honest person, and I treat my friends with respect," Lilia said.

"If you're such an honest person, then why did you promise to come to my performance and then just duck out in the end?" Joel asked in a harsh voice.

"I didn't duck out at the end. I did my best, Joel." The fact that Joel Zapata was the most handsome boy Lilia had ever known was becoming less and less important. His warm glowing eyes, his perfect features, the cute cleft in his chin, the curly black hair, all of it was fading into insignificance now that Lilia knew his offensive personality. Lilia had been flattered and interested when she had first met him, but now she was uncomfortable and angry.

"Well, I was really hurt when I looked out into the audience and I didn't see you," Joel said petulantly. "I wanted my girl to be right there up front."

"I'm not your girl, Joel," Lilia said. "We hardly know each other. And maybe it's best if we leave it like that."

Lilia turned and started walking away.

Joel leaped to her side, grabbing her hand. "Lilia, I'm sorry. I'm really sorry. Sometimes I do stupid things. I'm kind of brash sometimes. I forget I'm in the real world, and I need to be more considerate. I'm really sorry. Forgiven?" he asked, with a pleading look in his eyes.

"Yeah, sure, it's okay," Lilia said.

"Does that mean you'll go to the movies

with me on Friday?" he asked.

"I don't know. I'll have to see," Lilia said. She forced a smile and hurried off. Then she looked back and added, "I'll let you know tomorrow."

Lilia rushed to the bus stop and waited with her friends.

"Did you tell Joel off?" Meghan asked.

"Yeah, I told him I resented him lying to my friends," Lilia said.

"And then you guys made up, right?" Holly asked, giggling.

"No," Lilia said. "He's just weird. I mean, everything about him is weird. He's . . . I don't know . . . controlling or something."

It occurred to Lilia then, that in some spooky way, Joel Zapata was like Charlie Spann, the man across the street. Lilia remembered Ashley saying that Mr. Spann treated his wife and daughter like his subordinates. And in some ways, Joel treated Lilia like that. It was as if Joel thought he could drive off Lilia's friends without giving it a thought. He was obsessed with having all of her attention. He couldn't stand for her to be distracted by her friends or even her grandmother.

Lilia made up her mind to disengage from Joel. She would do it gently—as gently as she could. She didn't want to go out with him on Friday night, or ever. She had the fear that the more time she spent with him, the worse it would get. She would be like a fly hovering too close to the sticky web, eventually trapped by the threads and doomed.

....

That night at home, Lilia went to her room to work on a history report. When she got tired of looking at the computer screen for good Web sites, she went to the window and looked across the street.

A car she had not seen before, a sporty little red convertible, was in the driveway. After a few minutes Lilia saw Robert Spann, Cassidy's 18-year-old brother, walk from the house. He was a tall, studious-looking college boy with a strong resemblance to his father. Lilia remembered him from her freshman year at high school. He had just graduated from Agua Dulce last year and had gone off to a college about 70 miles away. Lilia had always liked Robert. He was a very nice guy.

Lilia ran down the stairs and dashed out the front door. Lilia called out to Robert, "Hi, Robert."

Robert smiled. "Hi, Lilia," he said.

Lilia drew closer and could see the deep sadness and worry on the young man's face.

"I'm sorry about your mom and sister," Lilia said. "It must be awful not knowing where they are."

Robert nodded. "Yeah, we're really worried," he said.

Lilia wondered if it ever crossed Robert's mind that his father had something to do with the disappearance of his mother and sister.

Suddenly the front door of the Spann house opened. Charlie Spann stood there, framed in the doorway, his face contorted with rage. "You rotten little troublemaker!" he screamed at Lilia. "What are you talking to my son for? Trying to poison him like you've poisoned everybody else?"

7 "IT'S ALL RIGHT, DAD," Robert said, acutely embarrassed.

"No, it's not all right," Mr. Spann yelled. "They—those nosy neighbors across the street—called the police on me. They told the police I had done something to your mother and sister. The police came here with dogs and turned my home upside down. It most decidedly is not all right!"

Robert looked totally miserable as Lilia turned and walked back to her house. She quickly closed the door behind her.

"What was all the yelling about?" Lilia's mother asked.

"Robert's home from college, and I said a few words to him. Then his father came out and started screaming at me," Lilia said. "He really hates us because we called the police."

Lilia had assumed that that was the last she would see of Robert Spann, but at about 7:45, there was a rap on the door.

Robert stood there.

Lilia's father opened the door. "Robert. Come on in," he said.

Robert Spann walked into the living room, and Lilia's mom brought out some coffee and cookies. Robert's gaze shifted to Lilia. "I'm sorry my dad yelled at you like that. He's under a lot of stress," Robert said.

"That's okay," Lilia replied.

"My dad went out," Robert continued. "He won't be home for a few hours. He's at a bar. I'm glad that he's out, because sitting in the house worrying isn't doing him any good. It's making him crazy. I've never seen him like this. He's aged about ten years in the past week."

"What do you think happened, Robert?" Lilia's father asked the young man as they drank coffee. Robert did not touch Lilia's mom's homemade chocolate chip cookies. He had always been thin, but now he looked absolutely haggard.

"Cass called me at the dorm that Tuesday night," Robert said. "She said there was a major argument going on. She said this might be it. Cass was crying, and I felt really bad for her. I didn't know what to do. I should have driven down immediately. I could kick myself for not doing that. But I just figured it would blow over like all the other fights. But this time I guess my mom had had enough."

"So, you think your mother and sister are hiding out somewhere?" Lilia's mother asked gently.

Robert nodded. "They have to be. What other explanation is there?" he asked.

"But don't you think your mother would at least call you, and let you know she and Cassidy are okay?" Lilia asked.

"I think," Robert swallowed hard as if his words came with great difficulty, "I think my mom is . . . you know, getting even with my dad for a lot of stuff that's gone down. If she called me, she knows I'd call him. She'd ask me not to, but she knows me well enough to understand that I couldn't resist. I don't like to see anybody suffering, and my dad is suffering big time."

"Robert, did you know your father got rid of your mom's car?" Lilia asked.

"Didn't he just put it in storage?" Robert asked.

"I don't think so," Lilia said. "And he

smashed her collection of Christmas elves from Bavaria. Smashed them all, then threw them in the trash . . . "

Robert looked startled. His eyes grew large in his thin face. "He smashed them? Are you sure?"

"I saw them," Lilia said. "They were pulverized. Like he hammered them."

Robert took a deep breath. "Dad said he packed them in boxes and put them in the attic because they reminded him of Mom," he said.

Neither Lilia nor her parents wanted to say anything to Robert about their darkest fears. Lilia kept thinking of Mr. Spann struggling with the heavy bag on that Tuesday night, but she didn't have the heart to mention that. It would be too cruel.

Robert spoke as he cradled the cup of coffee in his hands. "Dad called all the shots. Mom worked and made good money, but he was the boss. Nothing happened that he didn't want to happen. Nothing. They argued, but he always won . . . I guess she couldn't take it anymore . . ."

"I'm sorry, Robert," Lilia's mother said. "It must be hard for you."

"Yeah," Robert said. He took a big gulp of coffee and got up. "It's always been hard for me. And for Cass." He shook his head, thanked Lilia's mom for the coffee, and left.

After he was gone, Lilia's family looked at one another.

Lilia's mother was the first to say what everybody was thinking. "He doesn't seem to suspect any foul play."

"Well," Lilia's dad said, "he knows his parents better than we do. Maybe he's right . . ."

In the morning, before Lilia left for school, a florist pulled up in front of the Martinez house and delivered a beautiful bouquet of roses.

"Wow," Elvira cried, "look what you got, Lilia!"

"Those are so beautiful," Dina said. "Who are they from?"

Lilia pulled the note from the tiny envelope. It read: I like to leave them laughing. I'd do anything for a joke. But when my baby's mad at me, my poor old heart is broke. Friday? Please, please? J

Lilia's mother was standing in the doorway watching Lilia read her note. "You don't look too pleased, sweetie," she said.

"Oh, it's from Joel Zapata. He's a new student. He works as a comedian sometimes, and he really wants to hang out with me. He wants to take me to the movies on Friday, but I don't want to go," Lilia said.

"Is he ugly?" Elvira asked.

"No, he's not ugly. He's very handsome," Lilia said.

"Then go out with him, silly," Elvira advised.

"I don't know," Lilia said. She gently took the roses from the box and put them in water. They were beautiful.

Lilia did not see Joel at school until lunchtime when he joined Lilia and her friends.

"May I join you lovely señoritas?" he asked with mock courtesy.

"Sure," Lilia said.

"So . . . am I forgiven?" Joel asked. He glanced at Holly and Meghan and said, "She's mad at me for chasing you girls off yesterday so I could have some private time with her. I said I was sorry . . ."

"Thanks for the roses," Lilia said. "They were gorgeous."

"He sent you roses?" Holly gasped.

"Real roses?" Meghan asked.

"No," Joel said, "they were fake. Actually they were dandelions painted red." Then he laughed and looked right at Lilia. "Are we on for the movies Friday?"

Lilia did not want to go the movies with Joel, but he looked so sincere, so hopeful. She weakened. She didn't have the heart to refuse him. He had gone to all the trouble and expense of sending those roses. "I guess so," she said.

"Good!" Joel cried triumphantly.

....

When Lilia got home from school that same day, her father said, "Mr. Spann was driven away by two police officers. It did not appear that he was under arrest, but it did look serious."

"Is Robert still over there?" Lilia asked.

"No, he drove away right after you left this morning. I suppose he had to go back to college. What can he do around here?" Lilia's dad asked.

Lilia thought about Cassidy. Poor little Cassidy. She always seemed so quiet and sad. What could have happened to her after that bitter fight between her parents?

Since there was nobody home at the Spann house, Lilia walked across the street for another look. In some of the television movies she watched, an ordinary person like herself often stumbled upon an important clue the police somehow overlooked. Lilia knew that was unlikely, but still she stared at the Spann driveway, the flagstone walk, in search of a bloodstain or something.

As she was looking, an elderly man's voice said, "Awful business, huh?"

It was Ned Webster, who lived on the other side of the Spann house. Mr. Webster's wife had died last year, and he was aimless now, spending most of his time watching television or the neighbors.

"Yes, Mr. Webster. I wonder what happened to Mrs. Spann," Lilia said.

"And the girl," Mr. Webster said. "Don't forget her. She's gone too."

"I know," Lilia said. "What could have happened?"

"I believe I know," Mr. Webster said. "The police talked to me, you know. I guess they talked to everybody around here. Well, I told the officer what I saw that Tuesday night. And I told him what it meant too."

Lilia wondered if Mr. Webster had seen Mr. Spann dragging the heavy bag to his car too. "What do you mean, Mr. Webster?" she asked.

"Well, Spann was acting really suspicious. They'd been fighting again. Nothing new there. But then it got quiet, and he came out with a shovel and a pick axe and put it in the car. I figured right away that he'd be needing those tools for burying something, or someone," Mr. Webster said.

Lilia stared at the old man. She had not seen Mr. Spann putting the shovel and pick axe in the car. Maybe he did that before he hauled the heavy bag out and put it into the trunk.

"If you ask me, those two—Mrs. Spann and the girl—are under the ground. That's what I believe," Mr. Webster said, "and that's what I told the police officer."

8 "OH, MR. WEBSTER," Lilia said with a shudder. "I hope that's not true."

"Well, to tell you the truth, Lilia, I never liked the Spanns. Never liked either one of them. Emily and I were married for 50 years, and we never had a big fight. We'd argue sometimes, but we wouldn't be screaming like the Spanns were. It was bound to come to a bad end, and I believe it has," Mr. Webster said.

About an hour after Lilia got home, Mr. Spann pulled into his driveway. Lilia was thankful he had not seen her talking to Mr. Webster. Mr. Spann hurried into the house. He looked weary and disheveled, but he was obviously not yet under arrest.

"He's back, huh?" Lilia said regretfully to her father. She wanted him in police custody. It was scary with him living across the street as if nothing had happened. "I talked to Mr. Webster. He saw Mr. Spann putting a shovel and a pick axe in his car on Tuesday night. He thinks

Mrs. Spann and Cassidy are dead and buried."

"I hope not, but it sure is appearing more and more suspicious," Lilia's dad conceded.

Lilia went to her room to work on her history project. Elvira appeared in the doorway. "Lil, why don't the police take Mr. Spann away? It scares me that he's over there. I get nightmares. I'm scared he'll come over here and hurt us," she said.

"The police can't arrest him until they have some good evidence. You can't just arrest somebody and put them in jail until you find evidence against them," Lilia said.

Elvira seemed unconsoled by the explanation. "But I'm scared that he's over there and maybe he killed somebody," she said.

"Don't be scared, Elvira," Lilia said, smoothing the dark hair from her little sister's brow. "The police are watching his house. I see the unmarked cars parked down the street. If he does anything weird, they'll come in a hurry."

"Are you sure?" Elvira asked.

"Yes," Lilia said. "Anyway, even if he did hurt his wife, it was during a big fight. He wouldn't just come over here and bother us."

But, as Lilia tried to comfort her little sister, she was far from sure about what she was saying. She wasn't sure the police were watching the Spann house, and she didn't trust Mr. Spann. If he had committed a murder, he could strike again.

"I just wish they'd take him away," Elvira said.

"Elvira, we're not absolutely sure he did anything yet," Lilia said. "It could be that Mrs. Spann and Cassidy are hiding out somewhere."

"No," Elvira said. "He wouldn't have smashed the little elves if he knew she was coming back. One time Mrs. Spann invited me into her house when her husband wasn't home. She showed me some of the elves. They were so cute. She said she loved them more than she loved everything else in the house put together. If she had left, like he said she did, she would have taken the elves with her."

"Maybe she left in a big hurry and didn't

have time," Lilia said.

Soon after Elvira had gone to bed, Lilia put on her pajamas and brushed her teeth. Before climbing into bed she went to the window to watch the owls and to glance at the Spann house. It used to be a pleasant ritual to watch the white owls diving in the night. Now the ritual was stained with horror. Lilia couldn't look out her window anymore without being reminded of Mr. Spann walking, stumbling under the burden of that heavy bag.

....

"Be sure to wear something red on Friday," Joel told Lilia at lunch the next day. "You look so great in red with your dark hair and skin color. Red is your color."

Holly and Meghan were at the lunch table too, and Holly snickered at Joel's comment. "When did you ever see Lilia in red?" she asked. "She hates red."

"Yeah, that's true," Lilia said. "My favorite colors are blue and yellow. One time my aunt got me a red sweater, and I wore it to please her, but I never liked it."

"Trust me," Joel said. "Red is your color. I know these things. I guess I must have seen you standing against a red banner or something. You were smashing! I thought, wow, is that good or what? So maybe you could get a red pullover for Friday, huh?"

"I don't think so," Lilia said.

"I'd be so proud of you if you wore red just for me," Joel said.

"Joel," Holly said, "give it a rest, will you? You're making me crazy. Leave the girl alone!"

Holly and Meghan left the table first, leaving Lilia and Joel for a few more minutes before lunch period ended.

"Your girlfriend, Holly, has a nasty way about her, hasn't she?" Joel said. "She's just the kind of girl I hate. Princess of the put-downs. Hey, maybe I can work up a sketch about a girl like her. That should bring some laughs next time I go on. Hey, I might even use her real first name. Just the first name. I'm not eager to get sued, but it's really funny when some of the kids in the audience recognize who you're talking about."

Lilia didn't smile. "Holly is very nice. She doesn't put people down. It just was getting on her nerves how you were harping on that red stuff," she said.

A wide grin split Joel's face. "Let's see, during my act I could say, there's this chick, Holly . . . "

Lilia cut into Joel's words. "Joel, I hope you're joking. That would be a really cruel thing to do. Most of the kids at Club Jupiter know the other kids at Agua Dulce. That would be awful."

"Yeah, I'm only joking," Joel said. "I wouldn't do that unless I was really ticked off at somebody. One time I asked this girl for a date in my old high school before I came here, and she put me down in a really cold way. Well, I did a comedy sketch for the school talent show, and I put her on the griddle good. Everybody was laughing their heads off because nobody liked her. Man, I bet that was the worst night of her life."

Lilia sat there finishing her milk and thought, I really don't like you, Joel Zapata. I have tried very hard to like you, but I almost hate you. You are mean and controlling. There is no way in the world that I am going to the movies with you this Friday or any other time. But to Joel she said, "Oh, Joel, I forgot to tell you. Something came up, and I can't make the movies on Friday."

The smile vanished from his face. "It's because I insulted your friend, isn't it?" he demanded. "Now you're paying me back by canceling our date."

For just an instant Lilia considered making up some phony errand to explain why she couldn't go on Friday. But then she thought, hey, Lilia Martinez, do you have a backbone or what? So she said, "Joel, I don't like the way you deal with people, okay? To tell you the truth, you're a very talented guy. And some of your skits are hilarious, but I hate the undercurrent of meanness. I hate the way you seem to enjoy hurting people and embarrassing them. It's not fun for me to be with you, Joel."

"I'm sorry. I'm very sorry, okay?" he said.

"No, it's not okay. You're probably a very nice guy underneath that nasty, brash attitude, but I don't like being with you. Thanks for asking me to the movies, but I don't want to go. I don't want to date you at all," Lilia said.

Lilia walked away from the table, and Joel said, "Check this out. Lilia the lizard. There's this girl who reminds me of a reptile. She's cold and slinky. Now I'm not saying the girl is totally a lizard yet, but she spends too much time in the sun and yesterday I noticed somebody filing their nails on her cheek . . ."

Lilia walked faster, out of the lunchroom, away from Joel's laughter. Lilia played tennis a lot and she worried about having dry skin. She used a lot of lotions. But now she would wonder if the lotions were doing any good . . . Joel knew just how to hurt somebody.

"The creep," Lilia muttered to herself. "The little creep. And to think I even considered dating him!"

As Lilia rode the bus home from school that day, she thought about Charlie Spann. Even now, in his late forties, Mr. Spann was a handsome man. He was probably good-looking when he was young too. Just like Joel. Poor Connie probably fell in love with his looks and ignored the warning signals—the nasty, domineering personality. She married him, had two kids, and was stuck. She probably stayed in the marriage for the kids. With Robert in college and Cassidy a few years from there, she was almost home free. But she didn't quite make it.

When the bus turned down Lilia's street, Lilia was shocked to see police cars all over the place. Her first thought was that they had finally come to arrest Mr. Spann. She jumped off the bus and ran down her street. As she ran, she noticed her father standing in the yard.

"Dad! What's going on?" she cried.

"An hour ago," Lilia's father began, "Mr. Webster heard yelling over there, and he called 911. Somebody's injured. They're taking somebody out of the house."

Lilia turned numb. Somebody must have gone into the house to confront Mr. Spann, and he attacked them. But where was Mr. Spann?

9 "I HOPE THAT'S NOT ROBERT they're putting into the ambulance," Lilia's mother said. "Poor kid. Maybe he came back and got into an argument with his father."

"I don't see his car," Lilia said. "He drives that little red sports car. It's not in the driveway."

"Where's Mr. Spann?" Lilia's father asked the question that was on everybody's mind. It appeared that they had carried a victim out, but where was Mr. Spann? Everybody watched the door of the Spann house expectantly, waiting for a handcuffed Charlie to emerge.

"They'll probably bring him out soon," Lilia's mother said. "He can't wriggle out of this one. He'll be put under arrest, and then the police can find out what happened to Connie and Cassidy."

The person on the gurney was placed in the ambulance. Meanwhile, the police strung yellow crime scene tape all over the Spann yard. But the police did not lead Charlie Spann out of the house. A new fear arose from the gathered crowd.

"He must have gotten away," Mr. Webster said.

"Oh, that's the worst thing that could have happened," Lilia said. "That means he's on the loose out there. He could come back anytime."

"Yeah," Lilia's mom said, "we'd better be vigilant. Double-locked doors, and no wandering around at night."

The police at the scene were tight-lipped about what had happened in the Spann house. Eventually Lilia's father was able to get some information from a police officer he knew.

"Officer Waller, off the record," Lilia's father asked, "who got hurt in there?"

Officer Waller explained the situation to Lilia's father.

"Charlie Spann was the one on the gurney," Lilia's father said, after returning to the family with the information.

"What?" Lilia gasped. "But that's not possible!"

"They aren't saying what happened. He was arguing with somebody, and it got hot and heavy. Anyway, it looks like blunt force trauma, according to Officer Waller. He said somebody grabbed a poker from the fireplace and let Charlie have it. I guess he's is in pretty bad shape. Charlie might not even make it to the hospital," her father reported.

"What a horrible, horrible tragedy," Lilia's mother said, near tears. "To think we've known these people for years. We've had them over for barbecues. Lilia, you've gone to school with their kids. Sure, they were never my favorite neighbors, but they seemed ordinary—just ordinary people. How could something this dreadful have happened?"

It was a somber dinner that night at the Martinez home. Instead of the usual grace they said before each meal, Lilia's mother led a prayer for the Spann family.

"Is that guy across the street going to die?" Elvira asked as they began their meal. Lilia knew what was going through her little sister's mind. Elvira would feel better, safer, if Charlie Spann was really and truly dead. Lilia had the same feeling. She felt guilty to realize how relieved she was when she found out it was him on that gurney. At least there wasn't a madman loose in the neighborhood anymore. The madman had been struck down himself. But by whom?

"He probably is dead by now, or close to it," Lilia's father said.

"I wish it wouldn't have happened on our street," Dina said. She seemed to have lost her appetite for dinner.

"We don't get to choose where and when awful things happen," Lilia's mother said.

"At least it's over with," Elvira said. "Someone else will move into the house."

Who will want to? Lilia thought to herself. Move into a house where three people probably died violently?

That night on the late television news, the Spann story was featured. "A new and shocking development in the story of the disappearance of Connie Spann and her daughter, Cassidy," the anchor said. "After 15 days, the pair remains missing, but earlier today police were called to the house after sounds of an argument. They found Charlie Spann, husband and father of the missing persons, critically injured from what police are describing as blows to the head. Kathy Fenwick is standing live at Center Circle Hospital with an update. Kathy, what can you tell us?"

The news reporter on the scene appeared on the TV screen. "Thanks, Brooke. We have just attended a news conference where it was reported that Mr. Spann has died of his injuries," she said grimly. "As soon as more information is released we will bring it to you."

"Who could have gone in that house and done that?" Lilia's father wondered aloud.

Robert! Lilia thought, turning cold. It had to have been Robert. He must have put two and two together and confronted his father with his suspicions. Maybe there was a fight that led to Robert grabbing the iron poker and killing his father.

"You don't think it was Robert, do you?" Lilia's mother asked, expressing the thought that weighed heavily on Lilia's mind. "If it was him, nobody could blame him. The boy probably just lost it."

Robert's studious face came to Lilia's mind, and tears welled in her eyes. He had seemed so sad when he came to the house a few days ago. At the time, he seemed to completely accept his father's explanation that Connie and Cassidy were hiding somewhere. But perhaps recently he had discovered something that triggered rage.

Lilia didn't want to go to school the next day. She didn't feel like sitting in classes listening to why Samuel Tilden actually won the election of 1876, even though Rutherford B. Hayes was inaugurated president. She wasn't interested in reading a short story by Mark Twain about a frog that outjumped all the other frogs in a small California town. But she went to school anyway. She scarcely paid attention to anything she was hearing. She simply went through the motions. Then, at lunchtime, she and her friends listened to the radio.

The coroner's report on Charles Spann was not yet final, but his death was being considered a homicide. Lilia closed her eyes and thought about Robert Spann. She felt sure he had killed his father. Who else would have done it?

Little things about Robert Spann recurred in Lilia's mind, things she hadn't thought about in years. How he wrinkled his nose when he was puzzled, how he laughed so easily, how he helped out on that science field trip. He gently led the way in examining everything on the sand. He reminded everybody to be careful because the ecological system depended on all the creatures present.

"We mustn't remove anything that nature needs," he had said.

It was so hard to believe that gentle Robert had fatally struck his father. But then again, Lilia could only imagine the stress Robert must have been feeling.

At about 7:00 in the evening that night, Robert Spann's red convertible pulled into the driveway across the street. Lilia and her mother caught Robert before he went inside. Both of them hugged him.

"I'm so terribly sorry about your . . . losses, Robert," Lilia's mother said. "Let us know if there's anything we can do."

"Thank you," Robert said. He seemed like a man who was sleepwalking. There was a glazed look in his eyes as if he didn't quite comprehend the events of the past days. "There are papers I need in there . . . insurance . . . stuff like that," Robert said.

Lilia's father arrived then too. He put his hand on Robert's shoulder and said softly. "You can't go in there, Robert. It's a crime scene . . . the tape is stretched over the door."

The door to the Spann house opened, and two police officers stepped out. One of them looked at the boy and said, "You're Robert Spann, aren't you?"

"Yes, sir," Robert said.

Just then two detectives who had been sitting in an unmarked car watching the house from down the street approached. "Robert Spann, we need to talk to you," the older of the two said. "We wanted to talk to you at the hospital, but you left before we had a chance."

"I'm sorry," Robert said. "I didn't know."

"Would you come down to the police station with us now and answer a few questions?" the first detective asked.

"Yes, sure," Robert replied. He seemed

bewildered. He walked with the two detectives to their car, and all three got in. Robert was not under arrest. It was obvious though that he was a suspect, perhaps the only suspect they had. He was the only family member left to be a suspect.

It was not that Robert Spann had ever been Lilia's boyfriend, but he was a friend. He was a warm, familiar face in her growing-up years. He was a schoolmate, a guy she enjoyed sharing school projects with. He was the lanky kid across the street.

Many times she had seen him skateboarding along, doing daredevil stunts with homemade ramps leading from the curbs. Years ago during hot summers they bought orange ice pops and sat on the curb under a tree to enjoy them. He was just a nice kid. Things like this should not happen to nice kids. And just thinking about it caused tears to stream down Lilia's face.

Lilia's mother put her arm around her daughter's shoulders. "I know. It's sad. So sad."

"I hope there's some family for the boy to turn to," Lilia's dad said. "At 18 years old he shouldn't have to do that alone. I'm going to talk to my lawyer friend, Artie Olivares, tomorrow. Maybe he can do something to help Robert. Even if the boy did harm his father, the circumstances were horrendous. Artie is good at tracking people down too. If there are any relatives out there, he can find them, and make sure Robert isn't alone."

....

When Lilia woke up the next morning, she noticed Robert's red sports car still parked at the house. That meant the police had not driven him back to get his car. There were police officers going in and out of the house.

Lilia went to school and tried to focus, but she couldn't. After the day was over she couldn't remember anything from any class.

About 20 minutes after Lilia got home from school, a sedan pulled into the Spann driveway. From the license you could tell it was a rental car. A man about

70 was driving the sedan, and a woman about the same age was beside him. There were two people in the back of the sedan too.

"Mom!" Lilia screamed. "Dad! Mom! Come quick, look!"

Connie Spann walked between the older couple who were obviously her parents. Cassidy walked behind them. The four of them approached the Spann house.

10 LILIA AND HER MOTHER ran from their house.

"Cassidy!" Lilia screamed, "Oh, Cassidy, you're all right! We were all so worried!"

Cassidy turned stiffly and blinked. "Hi, Lilia," she said.

"Connie," Lilia's mother said, reaching out to the woman. "Are you okay? We were afraid something terrible had happened to you and Cassidy. It was all over the TV and the papers, and we feared the worst."

Connie nodded. "I know. I saw the television reports and the articles in the papers. I felt so guilty to be causing all that fuss. But Charles . . . he threatened me that night. He said I'd never be able to leave him—that he'd find me and drag me back. I am sorry for Robert and the pain I caused him. But Robert is such a softie. If I had called Robert, he would have told Charles everything," she said. The woman's face was drawn and haggard.

She looked like she was under tremendous strain.

"He got rid of your car and the elves," Lilia said. "We thought for sure you were dead when that happened."

The woman's eyes filled with tears. "He wanted to destroy everything I care about. He couldn't find me so he took it out on the elves. He knew that when I finally came back to get my things, it would hurt me to see everything gone. Even my clothes. He put all my clothing in a big bag and took it to the dump," she said.

That was what must have been in the heavy bag, Lilia suddenly realized. But how did Connie know that her husband had taken all her clothing to the dump? She had to have had some contact with him . . .

"So now your husband is gone," Lilia's mom said. "It's over."

"No, not quite," Mrs. Spann said. "The police are holding Robert. Can you believe such a thing? Poor sweet Robert who is so gentle he wouldn't even put out gopher traps when the rodents were destroying our yard. How ironic. Robert is down there answering their questions . . . after all he's been through."

"Is there anything we can do?" Lilia's mom asked. "All this must be so traumatic for you."

"Nothing could be as traumatic as the last 19 years," Mrs. Spann said. "Living with that man was like serving time in a prison. He was the warden. Every moment of my life had to be accounted for. And when I crossed him, he found a way to punish me. He drove my family away; he isolated me. He alienated all my friends. I had just one left, Vicky. I was hiding out with Vicky after I ran away. Thank goodness for her."

Cassidy had turned her face away, and she was crying in her grandmother's arms. Her grandfather looked nervously at her.

"If I had to list every mean little thing he ever did to me, I'd need a book the size of the telephone directory," Connie said. Then, abruptly, she stopped talking and followed the course of a police cruiser coming down the street. "There they are," she said.

Lilia wondered what she meant. Were the police bringing Robert back to his car?

Another thought came to Lilia's mind.

"Mrs. Spann?" a young officer asked as

he stepped from the squad car.

"Yes," she said. Mrs. Spann turned briefly toward Lilia and her mom. "I called the police on my cell phone on the way over here. I told them they should let my son go because he had nothing to do with what happened to his father. The truth is, I came over to the house alone Wednesday afternoon in hopes we could talk about the divorce in a civilized way. He taunted me about the clothing he had destroyed, how he smashed the elves and sold my car as junk. Then he struck me. I grabbed for the closest thing I could find to defend myself. It was the poker from the fireplace," she said.

She turned toward the police officer then and said, "I'm ready. Let's go."

....

At school on Monday, Lilia, Holly, and Meghan talked about the Spann case. Cassidy would not be returning to Agua Dulce. Her grandparents planned to enroll her in a private school until her mother's problems were settled.

"Mrs. Spann has a good lawyer," Lilia said. "My dad said she can probably plea bargain and get a suspended sentence. After all, it was self-defense . . . "

"Yeah," Holly said, "I'm betting she gets off completely if he was that awful to her."

"Uh-oh," Meghan whispered, "don't look now, but I think Joel is standing over there watching us . . . "

"I'm just going to ignore him," Lilia said.

"Are you two still together?" Meghan asked.

"Nope. I told him I never want to see him again," Lilia replied.

"Really? And no second thoughts?" Holly asked. "I mean, he's awfully good looking. You've got to give him that."

Lilia closed her eyes for a moment and it all swept before her mind like a movie—the tragic drama that Mrs. Spann had lived through. It had all started nicely enough, a girl enchanted by a handsome boy, ignoring the troubling little signs that he was cruel, harsh, and controlling. And it ended with the death and destruction of a family.

"No second thoughts," Lilia said, then, with even more feeling, "absolutely no second thoughts."